Norris

The Bear Who Shared

For Felicity x
C.R.

ORCHARD BOOKS

338 Euston Road, London NW1 3BH

Orchard Books Australia

17/207 Kent Street, Sydney, NSW 2000

First published in 2010 by Orchard Books
This edition published in paperback in 2010
ISBN 978 1 84616 309 8
Text and illustrations © Catherine Rayner 2010

The right of Catherine Rayner to be identified as
the author and illustrator of this work has been asserted
by her in accordance with the Copyrights,
Designs and Patents Act, 1988.

A CIP catalogue record for this book is available
from the British Library.

10 9 8 7 6 5 4 3 2 1

Printed in China

Orchard Books is a division of Hachette Children's Books,
an Hachette UK company.
www.hachette.co.uk

Norris
The
Bear
Who
Shared

Catherine Rayner

ORCHARD BOOKS

Norris

was wise.

And being a wise bear,
Norris knew that plorringes
were the best fruit of all.

So, wise Norris waited

under the plorringe tree –

he knew something special

would happen.

But Norris wasn't the **only** one
who **loved plorringes** . . .

. . . Tulip and Violet

loved them too.

They clambered closer to the plorringe

and gazed at it.

It looked delicious.

Wise Norris watched and waited . . .

Tulip and Violet
sniffed the plorringe.

It smelt of honey
and sunny days.

And Norris just waited.

Tulip and Violet
listened to the plorringe.

But it didn't make a sound.

Tulip and Violet
hugged the plorringe.
It felt as soft as candyfloss.

And all the while,
wise Norris waited.

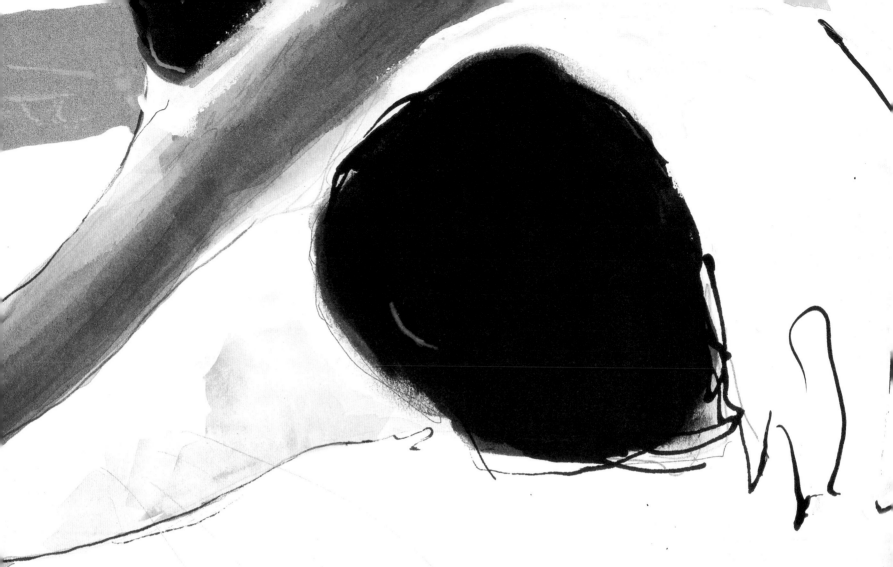

Tulip and Violet

were just about to have a little lick

of the plorringe, when . . .

UH-OH!

WHOMP!

Norris's wait was over.
The plorringe was his!

But what about Tulip and Violet?

Well, Norris was wise.
And he was also kind.

So, he shared the
delicious, sun-kissed,
soft-as-candyfloss
plorringe

with Violet

and Tulip too.

And Norris was right
(being wise, he was usually right),
a special thing had happened
under the plorringe tree . . . .

... Norris had
two new friends,
and from then on
they shared
everything.